A String of Beads

text by
Margarette S. Reid

pictures by
Ashley Wolff

· Dutton Children's Books ·

· New York ·

To my daughters, Heather and Laurel, and their dad, my husband, Jack

M. S. R.

For Madeline and all the Rooftop kids

A. W.

Text copyright © 1997 by Margarette S. Reid
Illustrations copyright © 1997 by Ashley Wolff

All rights reserved.

CIP Data is available.

Published in the United States 1997 by Dutton Children's Books,
a division of Penguin Books USA Inc.
375 Hudson Street, New York, New York 10014

Designed by Sara Reynolds and Semadar Megged
Printed in Hong Kong   First Edition
10 9 8 7 6 5 4 3 2 1   ISBN 0-525-45721-6

We're beaders, Grandma and I. We collect beads and make great necklaces together.

Beads are so cool. They come in
every color, size, and shape.

They're made of just about anything
by people who live all over the world.

Grandma and I like to sort beads together. We sort by colors first. Sometimes it's hard to tell if a bead is mostly red or mostly blue or definitely purple.

Next we take one set of colors and sort it again by shapes.
Grandma laughs at my shape names.

Beads that she calls disks, I call Frisbees.

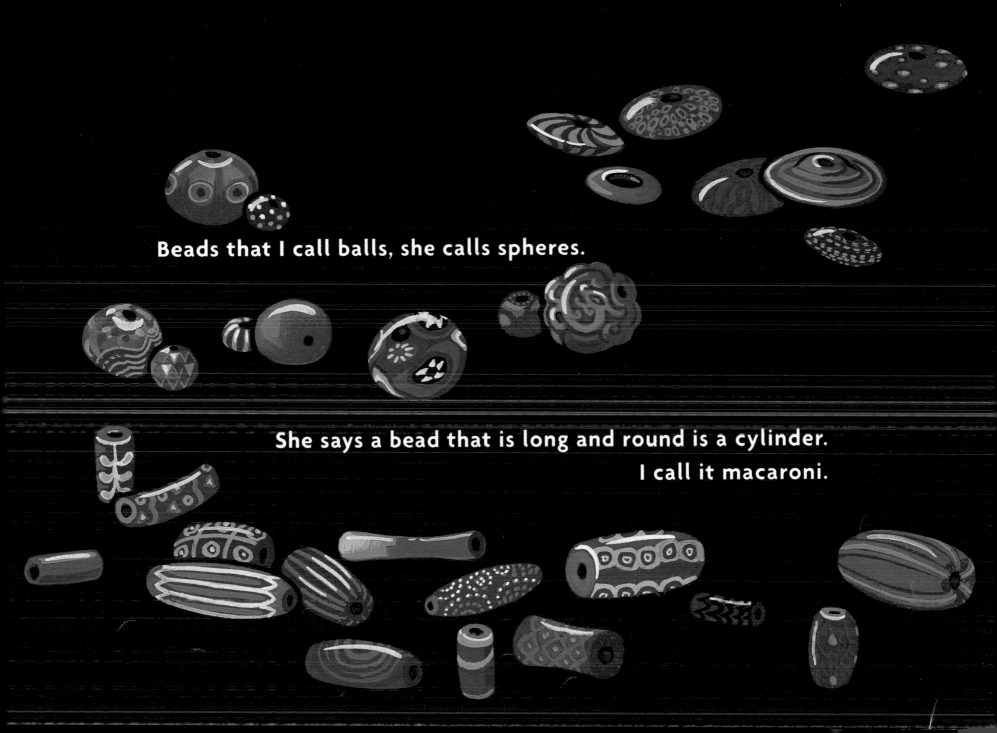

Beads that I call balls, she calls spheres.

She says a bead that is long and round is a cylinder.
I call it macaroni.

It's easy to separate little beads from big beads, but you have to line up the in-between ones to be sure.

Some small ones are called seed beads.
(They're not really seeds.)

Bugle beads are longer.
(They're not bugles, either.)

These five long blue beads equal ten round yellow beads or twenty red seed beads.

Grandma says Native Americans use bright-colored seed beads to weave pictures. They wear those beaded designs when they dress up for powwows and other special celebrations.

Animal? Vegetable? Mineral? Grandma and I play that game when we sort beads.

Some beads come from animals—from bones, teeth, claws, horns, and even eggshells.

Coral and shell beads come from animals that live in the sea.

Pearls form inside the shells of live oysters!

Beads made from plants are vegetable. Seeds and nuts and the wood of trees make beautiful beads.

"Do you know what these amber beads used to be?" Grandma asks. "Tree sap! Millions of years ago, the land was covered by oceans and even glaciers. The sap became a fossil." I think amber beads look like drops of sunshine.

Glass, stone, and metal beads are mineral.

Some special glass beads are called *millefiori*.
It means "a thousand flowers."

Glass beads with facets sparkle
like precious jewels. All their little sides,
or faces, catch the light.

Native Americans carve beads shaped like animals from pretty colored stones. They're called fetishes.

Gold and silver are metals that can be made into really fancy beads.

"It's the hole that makes a bead a bead, isn't it?"
I ask Grandma.

"You bet," she says.

"When were beads invented?" I ask.

"Beads are as old as the hills," she answers.

"That means nobody knows," I say, and we both laugh.

"Maybe long ago a kid like me found something that already had a hole in it, and she hung it on a skinny vine. Maybe when her friends saw that first bead, they went looking for things with holes, too."

"I like that story," Grandma says. "You know, all over the world, people traded things they had for other things they wanted. Since beads were small and easy to carry, merchants took them everywhere they went. They used beads the way we use money."

"Some Native American tribes made special beads from pieces of clamshells," Grandma tells me. "They called these purple-and-white beads wampum. Wampum belts were used to seal treaties and pledge peace."

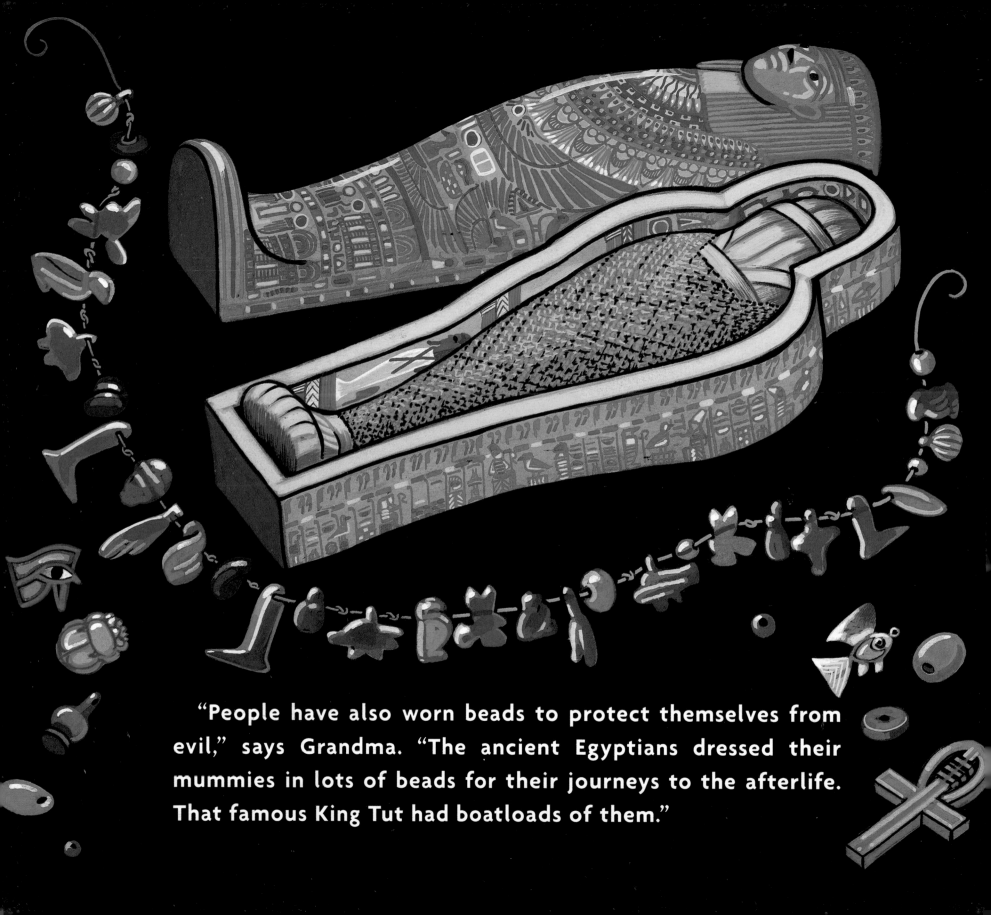

"People have also worn beads to protect themselves from evil," says Grandma. "The ancient Egyptians dressed their mummies in lots of beads for their journeys to the afterlife. That famous King Tut had boatloads of them."

"Since early times, people have touched beads as they said their prayers," she says. "Beads have always made people feel safe and important and beautiful."

Before I start a necklace, I check out our special beads. We
have ten silver ones

and seven millefiori

and five real turquoise beads.

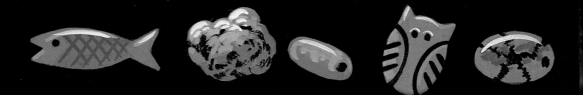

My favorites are eye beads. We only have four of those.

We have one face bead. I like how it looks.

Making a necklace means making lots of choices. Usually I put a big bead in the center of a string. On either side I line up other beads. Long and short beads, light and dark beads, smooth and bumpy beads. I match them and march them, two by two, to the ends of the string.

Once I made a necklace where every bead was different.

Sometimes I string a pattern of beads over and over.

Or change the order of beads I've chosen to make different patterns.

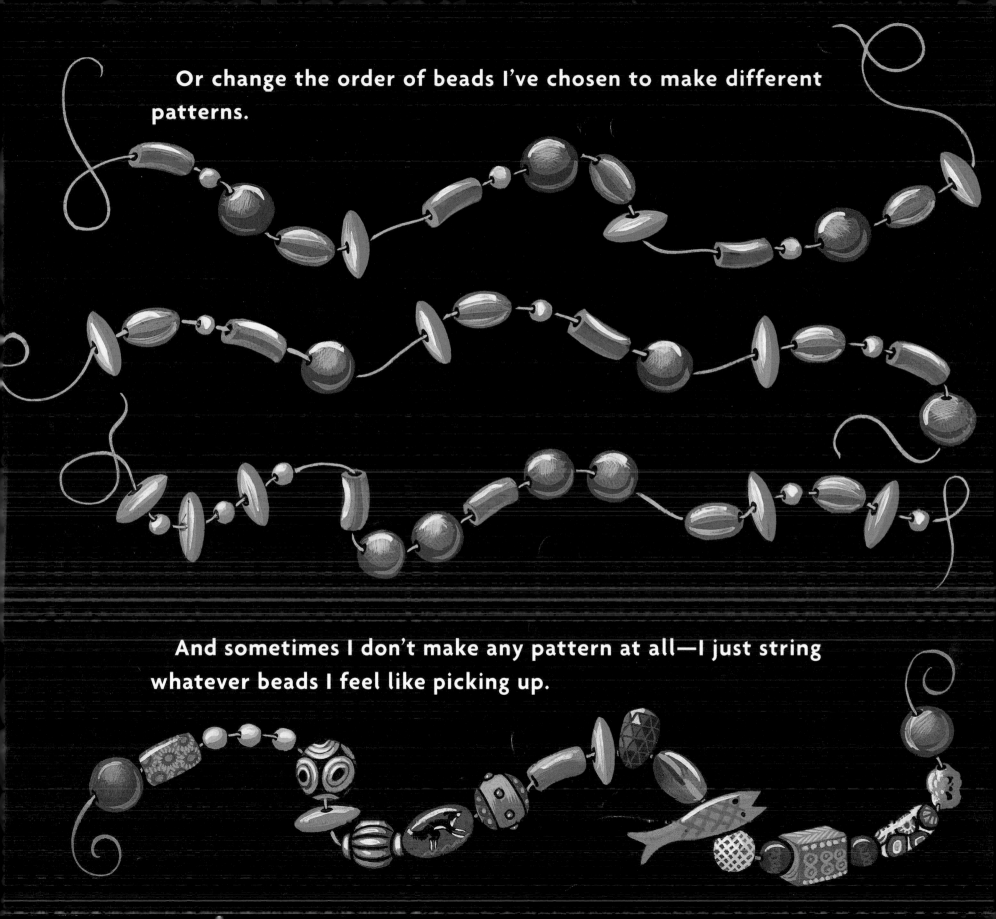

And sometimes I don't make any pattern at all—I just string whatever beads I feel like picking up.

"Oops!" I say when beads spill or a necklace breaks.
"Don't worry," Grandma says. "We can restring them. A necklace
may break, but beads are forever."

Sometimes the kids at my brother's play school ask me to help them make necklaces. We dye pasta with food coloring. Then we make presents for our moms and other special grown-ups. We make bracelets and anklets and ponytail holders for each other. I tie the knots in the elastic for the kids who don't know how.

Grandma shows me how to make beads from special clay
that she calls polymer.
We squeeze the clay to warm it.
Then we pull it and stretch it.

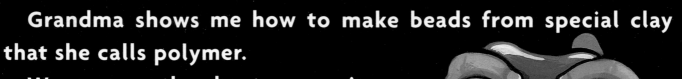

When we put two colors together,
it's fun to see the colors swirl.

We make fat logs

and thin snakes

and balls the size of marbles.

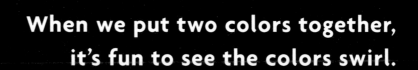

Sometimes I wrap two bright-colored snakes around each
other and twist them so I can make striped beads. They look
like candy caterpillars.

Sometimes I roll a caterpillar on the table to make smooth, thin beads.

Once I wound it around a pencil to make a fat coil bead.

Another time I made it look like a snail shell.

Grandma cuts the clay into bead lengths with a sharp, thin knife.

I make the holes with a toothpick.

When we bake them in an oven, our beads turn rock hard.

Guess who loves to wear all the things we make?

Everybody!

Here is more information about beads.

- Beads probably were first made at about the same time in different places around the world. The oldest ones discovered so far were found in France. They were made from animal teeth and bones about forty thousand years ago.
- Beads from kangaroo bones have been discovered in Australia.
- In caves in Korea, people have found very old beads made from deer toe bones.
- Disk-shaped beads made from fossil dinosaur and ostrich eggshells were found in the Gobi desert in Asia.
- Bones from fish and snakes have natural holes that make them easy to string. Many early peoples used them as beads.
- We know beads were important to people who lived long ago because we find beads in their graves. In South America, strings of tiny lizard-egg beads were found along with gold jewelry in clay pots.
- A wall painting in an Egyptian tomb shows craftsmen making, drilling, and stringing beads. Everyone, including pets, wore beads in Egypt. They thought beads brought them luck. *Sha* means "luck" in Egyptian, and *shasha* is the Egyptian word for *bead*.
- As early people moved around to find food, they carried beads with them. Wherever they went, they picked up new ideas about how to make and use beads.
- For thousands of years, up to the present day, people in

● Myth and mystery have grown up around certain beads. In Qom, Iran, people hang large, turquoise-colored beads around their donkeys' necks to protect them. Eye beads and face beads are believed to have the power to protect their wearers from evil. Those who wear Bodom beads—beads that are usually yellow with black or dark-gray inner cores—expect the beads to bark to warn them of danger!

● Native American women who were skilled at embroidering clothing with porcupine quills eagerly traded furs for bright-colored seed beads. The explorers Lewis and Clark wrote in their journals that they must be careful to keep enough beads in reserve to trade for food supplies on their return trip.

● Japanese artists carve delicate bead sculptures of fruit, flowers, butterflies, and even dragons from a smooth, hard stone called jade—and also from peach stones!

● Today in Africa, as in the past, village craftsmen specialize in making beads from the materials they find around them. The Dogan of Mali make granite beads. In Mauritania, glass is recycled by crushing bottles to make beads that have a soft, grainy look. The Turkana people make aluminum beads, sometimes by melting down cooking pots and pans. In Kenya, it is the custom for a woman who is waiting for her baby to be born to wear an amulet made from large, shiny brown beans. In Malawi, bright red and black beans make beautiful beads. They look delicious, but they are poisonous, so don't eat them!

● You can make beads from ordinary things around you— seeds, shells, acorn caps, paper straws, pasta, even buttons— just about anything you can string.

● All over the world, for as long as we can remember, people have loved beads and treasured them.

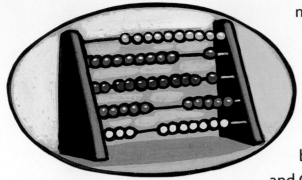

many countries used a calculator made of beads to keep track of what they bought and sold. It is called an abacus. Abacus beads are usually made of wood.

● The English word *bead* comes from the Anglo-Saxon *bede*, meaning "prayer." Prayer beads are used by Hindus, Buddhists, Muslims, and Christians. Although the beads are different, their purpose is the same: to guide worshipers through daily prayers.

● Around the time of Columbus, in the city of Venice, Italy, craftsmen made wonderful glass beads. To keep their methods secret, all Venetian bead makers had to live and work on one island. Although the craftsmen were threatened with death if they tried to leave that island, the secret was impossible to keep. Other centers sprang up to supply the growing demand for beads.

● Animals such as elephants and walruses that once provided ivory from their tusks are now protected. The tagua nut is an ivory look-alike that can be used for beads. It grows in the rain forests of Ecuador in South America.

● Ever since the first pearl was found inside an oyster, people have prized pearl beads. But until two hundred years ago, people didn't know how they were formed. Some people thought that oysters swallowed raindrops. Now we know that when a grain of sand gets inside an oyster's shell, the oyster coats it with layers of smooth, lustrous material called nacre. Behold—a pearl!